# The Story of CREATION

Illustrated by Pascale Lafond

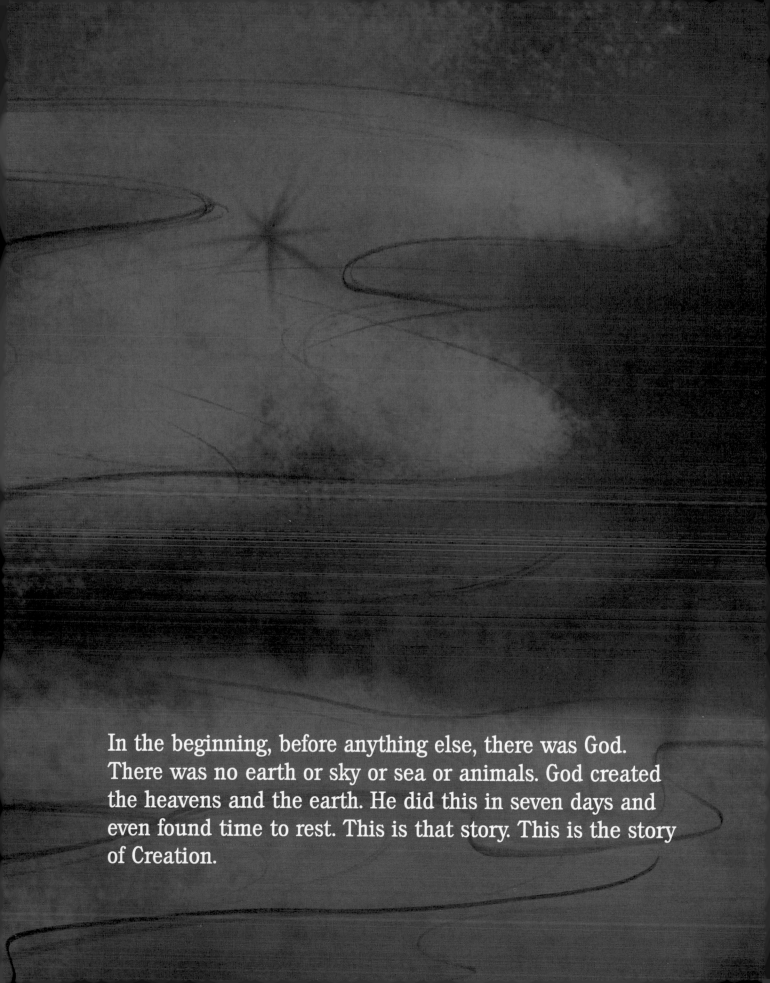

In the beginning, before anything else, there was God. There was no earth or sky or sea or animals. God created the heavens and the earth. He did this in seven days and even found time to rest. This is that story. This is the story of Creation.

God spoke into the darkness, "Let there be light!" And right away there was light which scattered the darkness. "That's good!" said God. He called the light day, and the darkness He called night. The evening came, the night passed, and the light returned.

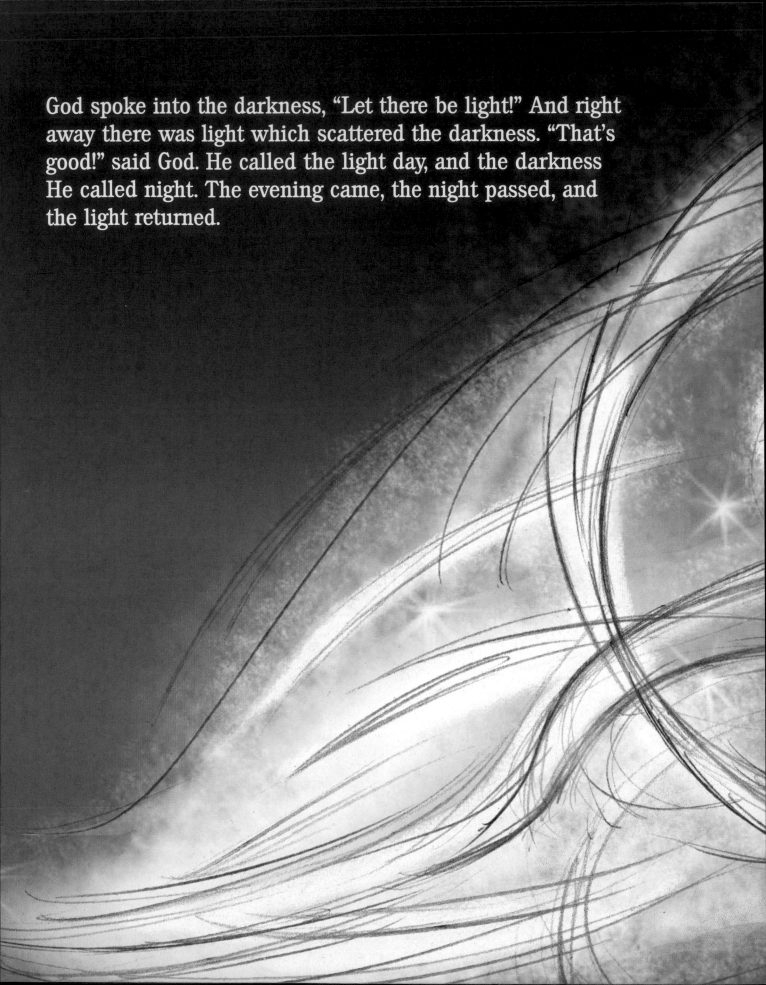

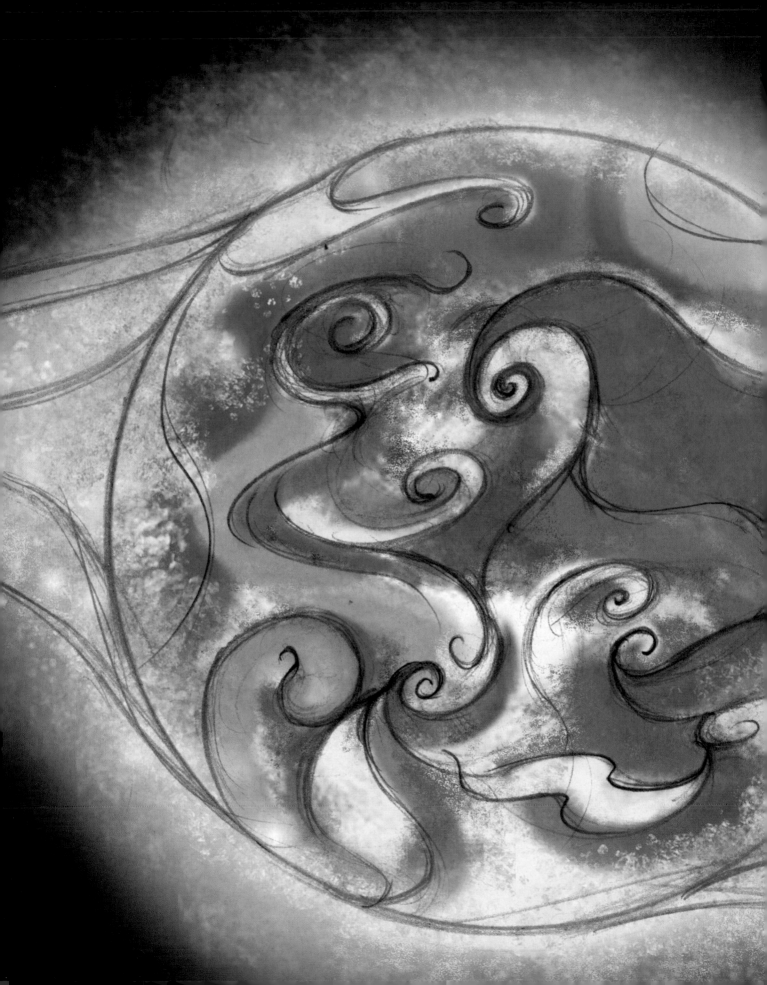

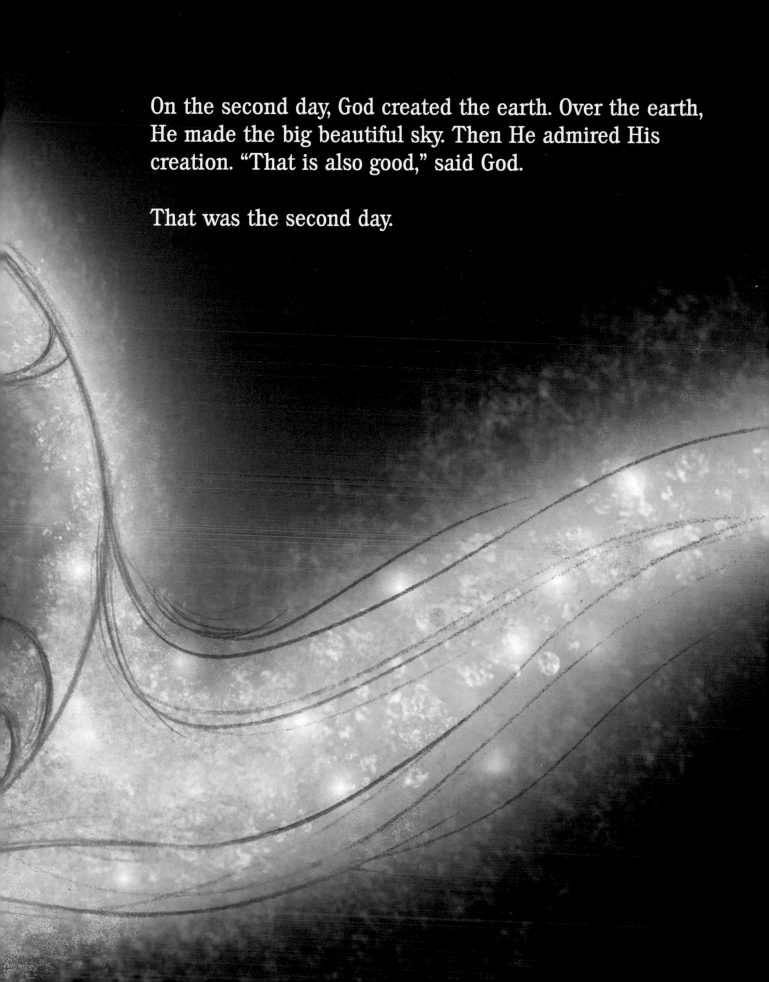

On the second day, God created the earth. Over the earth, He made the big beautiful sky. Then He admired His creation. "That is also good," said God.

That was the second day.

On the third day, God decided to organize the earth. God divided the earth into water and land. The dry land He called earth. The waters He called seas. God saw that it was good.

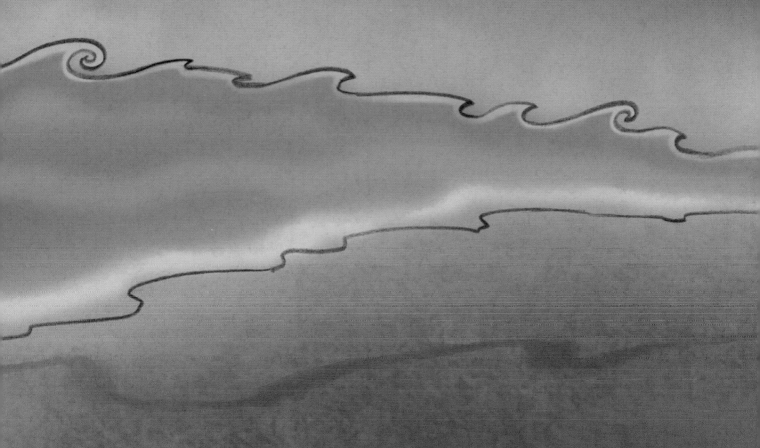

On this third day, God also created grass, plants, seeds, and trees to fill the earth. He called them forth, and they spread throughout the earth. And God saw that it, too, was good.

That was the third day.

Then God turned His attention to the sky. He made the sun and the moon. He made the stars and all the other planets. God made the sun to rule over the day and the moon to rule over the night.

God also used the sun, the stars, the moon, and the other planets to make the seasons. His creations would be signs to mark the seasons, days, and years on earth.

That was the fourth day.

On the fifth day, God went to work on the seas and the sky. He first turned to the seas and said, "Let them be filled with life." And they were.

He created millions of
little fish and countless
great whales. The
seas were alive
with life.

God also created birds on this day. He created birds of all kinds to fill the skies with their beauty and song.

God looked out over the skies filled with birds and seas filled with fish and saw that it was good. He blessed them all saying, "Be fruitful and multiply, and fill the waters of the seas, and let birds multiply upon the earth."

That was the fifth day.

On the sixth day, God made animals and every other living creature on the land. He made lions, tigers, dogs and cats. He made bugs, snakes, monkeys and mice. He made all of the creatures all over the world.

God filled every nook and cranny of the jungles of the world.

God filled the wide-open spaces on the prairies of the world.

And God saw that it was all good.

And then God made man and woman. God made us in His image. He gave us power over the other creatures of the world. He granted us dominion over the fish in the sea, the birds in the air, and every living thing that moved upon the earth.

God said, "Behold, I have given you all of this; the plants and animals, the fish and the birds, and everything full of life. Go forth and live."

God saw all that He had made, and it was good. It was very good.

That was the sixth day.

On the seventh day, God rested.

The earth and all living things are a great gift from God. We were given a great gift in life, and were given great responsibility as God's creation. God tells us to live in love for Him, for one another, and for His planet. His big beautiful planet. And it is good.